Other books by the Author:

And Mother came too
Why did you bring Mother?
Raspberry & Turner
Annie Butcher's Jigsaw
Annie Tries not to & Annie's Case Book

ANNIE'S
HAUNTING MEMOIRS
and
THE ABC
DETECTIVE AGENCY

JOY REID

Illustrations by Sue Millar-Smith

 www.trafford.com

North America & international
toll-free: 1 888 232 4444 (USA & Canada)
phone: 250 383 6864 ♦ fax: 812 355 4082

To all my family with love

Annie's 'Haunting' Memoirs

Joy Reid

CHARACTERS

Annie Butcher	Teacher of Biology at the 'George Pound' School
Sally Butcher	Annie's daughter
Bob	Sally's partner
Maggie Hurst	Head of the George Pound School
Lance Hurst	Maggie's husband
Philip	}
Jane	} the Hurst children
Pat	}
Sam	}
Dudley Russell	} old friends of Annie
Rose Russell	}
Alf	an old man who once lived opposite to Annie
Bert	a plumber
Kevin	Bert's son and still at school
Clare	an old-fashioned matron of the local hospital
John Watson	Clare's admirer
Neil LaCoste	Chief Inspector of Police in charge of investigation of International gang and admirer of Annie

Inspector David (and wife Eileen) due for retirement shortly

Sergeant Tracy Williams Rough and ready police sergeant, rides a motorbike

'Toy Boy'   A mysterious stranger lodging in the village

4

CHAPTER 1

Lance's Legacy

"**Y**OU LOOK PATHETIC HOBBLING DOWN the drive with that stick," said Maggie Hurst, Head of the George Pound School, to her friend Annie Butcher. "And what's more it gets in the way in the car. When are you getting your new one?"

"Stick or car?" answered Annie. She had already ordered the new car 'and about time' she thought. The new automatic car would be perfect for a disabled driver, her broken leg was mending, she would not be disabled for much longer and no longer have to listen to Maggie in a bad mood (this was unusual so what was up?) She kept silent and waited.

"Sorry," said Maggie, "I've a bit of a problem—it's Lance."

It would be Lance, thought Annie, it always was. Maggie's husband was Head of Music at the College. So much was going on in the educational world; there had even been a suggestion that the College might gain the status of a University. Certainly the George Pound might well be called an 'Academy'. But all these problems would be discussed in school whereas home problems . . . Annie sighed. Lance didn't mean to be trouble but he always was a bit of an enigma.

"Come to supper," said Maggie. "You can hobble that far, then I can tell you at leisure. I need your wisdom."

"Great, I'll come," replied Annie. "Whose turn is it to cook?" But Maggie had already started on the story.

"I'll tell you more tonight," she said as she dropped Annie off at The Lilacs. "Come early," she said.

Annie did and heard the story again from Maggie.

It was at breakfast when Lance had opened an official looking envelope. He gave a startled exclamation. "Would you believe it," he then said.

"What?" asked Maggie.

"Anything up, Pa?" asked Jane.

"Would you believe it," Lance repeated. "Great Uncle George has left me a house." Comments came quick and fast, a house? The children were fascinated.

"Who is Great Uncle George?"

"Why?"

"Where is it?"

"Why you?"

"I never knew we had a great Uncle George."

"Great, Great Uncle to you, Dummy!"

"Can we see it?"

Breakfast time during the term was not a time for long discussions so Lance, getting up, said, "It's called Greenwood Manor, not too far away. He probably left it to me as all other relatives are miles away, some in New Zealand. I expect he thought we could deal with it. We'll go and see it on Saturday—oh, that's tomorrow—right?" How much was true?

He kissed his wife 'goodbye' and was off.

"So," said Maggie to Annie, you know as much as I do. Can you join us tomorrow? I'll pick you up."

Annie was interested enough to say yes but she was full of her own news and no longer needed lifts for her new car had come. She was independent once more. She would be at Greenwood Manor on Saturday, but driving herself.

When Annie had been house hunting she had become fairly well acquainted with the local countryside and its houses but she was surprised at the size and beauty of Greenwood Manor when she was viewing it in a less detached way. Also it was not so far out as she had remembered. Lance was stressing this angle and Maggie had confessed to Annie that Lance had the ridiculous idea of their moving to it. One thing was absolutely sure, Maggie had said, and that was her determination not to!

Annie was followed by Dudley as she drove up to the imposing front. The Hursts were just in front, it was a small convoy.

The young people were almost silent as they climbed out of the car.

"Is this it?" Philip asked in tones of awe.

"It isn't anywhere else is it?" his twin told him. Sam said nothing at all, just stared and Pat thought of every word she knew to express her surprise and admiration.

"Not a hope," said Maggie firmly.

Annie could now see that it was in sad need of repair or even renovation.

"He probably had the income to go with it," Maggie was saying with a sniff.

Dudley had disappeared round the back. Annie was suspicious, this assembly had a contrived feel to it. Dudley, for one thing, had obviously been here before. Perhaps it was all innocent, perhaps Lance had often been kind and visited a lonely old uncle, or perhaps not.

"You know it's haunted?" asked Dudley as he left, "No-one will come near the place."

They went inside.

There was a pleasant hall with huge open fireplace but no fire had been burned there for many a year.

"Imagine," said Maggie in horror, "trying to find enough wood to keep it going," she turned from it to cut out its very existence. On the other side, opposite the fireplace was a wide staircase curving round at the top to two landings.

"Rather beautiful," said Annie, to be met by a glance of hostility from Maggie.

"Let's go up," said Jane.

"Come and look," called Sam from the large vaulted room to which the entrance hall led. They followed him in, aroused by the urgency in his voice. The room was empty except for a large concert grand piano. Even Lance looked startled. But, thought Annie, perhaps he had expected it to have been removed. From an insignificant door at the side of the room Dudley suddenly appeared.

"Ah ha!" he said.

"Ah what?" asked Maggie.

"It explains about the ghost," said Dudley. No-one ever sees anyone by day, but they hear the ghostly music at night."

"A ghost?" asked Annie.

"A little girl went missing, six she was and very pretty, her parents say she is still alive but the village says it's her ghost. There's a lodger at a friend's house. Everyone says he abducted her but he's still there so he can't have."

Annie agreed with him but she was vaguely uneasy.

Sam was gazing into the open piano admiring the strings. "It's beautiful," he said. "Could I learn to play it?"

Lance was silent, he offered no explanation, gave no comment on phantom melodies. He was suffering from mixed emotions, the strongest being the possible joy of one of his brood turning out to be musical.

"It must belong to Victoria Wood," ventured Sam. "She has a large piano, she must put it somewhere."

His theory was ignored.

"Do what?" he asked his father. "Let's do it!" he explained

"Learn to play the piano?" Lance replied, "It's more difficult than a recorder. First adjust your seat for height and comfort."

They looked around—no height or comfort. No, one lesson ruined and Sam, losing interest, went to join his siblings.

But Dudley must be listened to. He spoke to Maggie, he obviously expected them to follow him with gasps of pleasure at the sight of the old-fashioned staff quarters but there was no enthusiasm and nobody stirred.

Jane said, "Come on twin, let's go upstairs," they returned to the ante-room with the fireplace and enticing looking stairway. "We can decide on our rooms!" Philip and Pat followed her up to the bedrooms.

'No chance of a ghost with this lot around!' thought Annie.

Maggie looked round for somewhere to sit. Nothing was going to persuade her to visit more of the establishment but there was nothing. Dudley, seeing her predicament, left hurriedly and returned carrying a once-had-been embroidered piano stool. "Sorry," he said apologetically, "nothing to stand on out there. He paused to think up an excuse, "And lots of things to do if we are to get this place in running order."

Giving him anything but a grateful look, Maggie took the proffered seat into the entrance hall, to await the return of the first floor explorers.

Lance offered no comment, but he did think he might buy a short ladder for Dud's activities.

"When did Great Uncle George die?" Annie asked him, she had been an onlooker for some time. Perhaps his was this 'ghost'.

"Sev . . . ," Lance began and added, "Why don't you go home?"

"Not for worlds," retorted Annie as she joined Maggie.

"Nothing to laugh about," said Maggie crossly.

"Tell me about it," Annie said, continuing to enjoy the goings on in her own way. 'It's no good,' she told herself. 'I have to know the ins and outs of a case! It's all so contrived—there's nothing real, certainly no ghost.'

The bedroom party came clattering down the stairs full of bounce. "There are hundreds of bedrooms!" from Jane.

"Not exactly hundreds but enough for two each," from Philip.

"Two each!" Maggie cried. "Why? When you can't even keep one tidy?"

"It's because we don't have room for our things, we've a lot of clobber," Jane told her.

"There's plenty of room for Andrew," said Pat, "or all the Bushells when they come!"

"Dad," said Philip, "come and see the garden, we've looked at it from upstairs and there's masses of it."

Annie left Maggie's side as Dudley brought in a cup of tea and she joined the others in the garden. She, too, had looked at the grounds and was looking forward to imagining its restoration.

At the end of this large apartment there was a fairly modern French window. It led to an overgrown but more recently cleared patch. "Perfect for the swimming pool," said Pat and the others agreed with her.

"Could we have a picnic next week?" Jane and Philip asked in unison.

Annie noticed that they spoke to their Father. Maggie's unyielding look was not promising, she sat and pretended it was nothing to do with her.

"We'll tell them to bring their own food, then Mum won't have to worry about it."

"Some will, some won't, Saturday's okay by me," Lance added as Annie muttered 'five loaves and two small fishes.'

Dudley, appearing unexpectedly round the corner, had one of his bright ideas. "Tell you what, I'll build a barbecue, how about that?"

"Cool!" "Huge Man!" "Brill!" "Fantastic!" greeted this suggestion as they looked around for a suitable site.

"Yes, I'm going," Annie told Lance. "I've lots to do back home."

"You'll come next week won't you?" Sam asked her.

"Nothing, but nothing, would induce me to miss it," Annie replied, "and I shall bring my own food."

She left them and went for her car shouting to Dudley, "Don't forget the car park," as she drove away.

CHAPTER 2

The Picnic

THERE WERE MORE CARS THAN Annie had anticipated. Dudley had listened to her, it was well organized with 'WAY IN' and 'WAY OUT' signs. More cars meant more people so this looked like being a big event. She hadn't hurried and it was well underway. The first person she met was Rose pushing Victoria in a large and luxurious pram.

"There's a bit of a 'goings on' here, Rose explained, but I expect you know all about it. Is that your new car?" she went on. "Are you parking HERE?"

"Yes to the car, No to everything else," replied Annie. "I have my own parking space round the back." Had she?

Dudley has built a beautiful barbecue," Rose chatted on, "helped by your Australians. We were told to bring things to cook."

This was not as Annie knew it but things get altered with time but (and it was a large BUT), who were her Australians? She decided not to ask in case she didn't know any. Seeing Rose looking from small car to large pram and thinking the walk would do Rose good, she said, "See you later," and drove on.

Dudley had chosen the perfect spot for the barbecue, everyone had cleared the brushwood on the left of the TO-BE pool space. This space had been decided upon as it led from the main room. (The concert hall as Sam pointed out) the piano was still very much in evidence but a few boxes had been added for seating accommodation.

There was a queue at the BBQ over which Dudley presided. Annie went over to him.

"I've only got sandwiches," she said. "I didn't realize"

"Plenty of food, don't worry, what do you fancy?"

Dudley had two helpers, a man and a woman both unknown to Annie. They seemed very much at home here. It was a man who answered her, Dudley was busy tossing up some pancakes (or similar).

"There you are dear, don't worry, plenty of food."

He sounded very English, certainly not Australian. He introduced himself, "I'm Jason and my partner there is Kath. We like that place of yours and we'd look after it. Sold up you see, to go out there and didn't fancy it did we Kath?"

Annie didn't reply at once, who had even suggested that she might be interested. It was the problem that interested her. Of course there was no question of her moving elsewhere.

He broke in on her thoughts, "We'd pay the proper rate of course, use an agent if you like."

If I only knew what he is talking about, agent, rates? Perhaps he thinks I'm someone else, he spoke as if they'd known each other for years.

She accepted a plate of food and went to find a quiet place from where she could observe, think and hopefully, not be disturbed.

Maggie abandoned her stool and, seeing Annie looking peaceful in a quiet spot, joined her.

Annie patted the ground beside her, "Have some food," she said, "I've got much too much."

"Later," replied Maggie. "I'm not hungry anyway."

"Beautiful here isn't it?" suggested Annie tactlessly. "Tell me," she asked, "who are the very English Australians?"

"Helping Dudley? Don't you remember? The Denison's two children at school, decided to emigrate.

So they did know me, thought Annie, but that doesn't explain the 'agent' or 'rate'. It will explain itself meanwhile, enjoy this day. She relaxed.

Music could be heard, it would be coming through the open doors. It was the piano and it was being played by the hands of an expert.

"I'd better find myself some food," Maggie muttered and departed towards the house.

Lance could play almost any instrument and make it 'talk' but the piano was his favourite and now he was giving it all he'd got.

Maggie, listening, went to the open patio doors and leant there. Suddenly she was miles and years away—a young Maggie Browne watching the new handsome music lecturer. How could it happen? Why did it happen? How could a sensible student fall there and then so helplessly in love? If only she could stop breathing now at this blissful and unbelievable moment. He had looked up, there were other students there but it was at her he looked, and so it had continued—the wonder of it.

Now, Maggie stood there and felt the old emotions flow over her, even nearly twenty years and four children later.

Lance stood up and she walked into his arms. "We shall need more furniture," she said.

Annie heard the music stop, it seemed vey peaceful considering half the school seemed to be there—that is half the school and their parents. She fed the birds with the remains of her lunch. She hoped it would be found by birds—it could be anything. This wasn't a bad way of spending a warm Saturday.

She was found by Dudley. "There you are," he said, "Could you give Rose a lift home?"

"No," replied Annie, thinking of the size of her car and the large pram.

"I'll take the vehicle," Dudley told her, "It's just Rose and Vicky."

"Yes to that then, but tell me is there anywhere to get a cup of tea?"

"Of course, I've got tea going in one of the cottages. I'm doing one up for Alf if we can get him to move. It would suit Bert as well. Come and have a look."

Annie followed him. It had been a row of cottages but 3 small ones had been knocked into one, it was in here that tea was brewing and work was very obviously in progress.

"Bet will love this," Dudley told her, "and there's plenty of room for that lad of his and his friends. Now, "he continued, "how about this end one for Alf—perfect isn't it?"

Annie agreed—the cottage, although attached to the others, had a good view of the house activities as well as a good open view of the countryside. "Yes, perfect for Alf, he'll love it," she assured Dudley.

"What about you," she asked him.

"I'm perfectly happy where we are and I've some lovely workshops here."

Annie decided not to probe too deeply and she was disturbed when Dudley said, "Now," with emphasis, "Come and look at this."

This was a former lodge before the grounds had been extended. It was on its own with a small and pretty garden, well looked after.

Some students of Dr Hurst's were living here," he explained disapprovingly, "But the bargain was that they looked after the place. Suit you a treat wouldn't it?"

Annie recognized a plot when she came across one. The trouble with this one was that she had somehow come in at the wrong place. It had been spoilt by 'her Australians' who had their eyes on renting her bungalow. The beginning of Dudley showing her the lodge was now at the end. She needed a day or two, or three, or four, to make such a big decision.

It was Maggie who sorted it out for her. "We thought we'd give it a trial run for a year. Herr Gebhart wanted to bring his family over for a year, he wants his children to speak English. He asked if we knew of anywhere he could rent for a year, it just seemed convenient. It'll be fun at the Manor for that time. Do say you'll take the 'Lodge' and come with us."

CHAPTER 3

A S ANNIE SAT ON THE small patio outside the 'Lodge' and looked over the valley she thought how easy the move had been, it was rather obviously well thought out and organized. She was glad now that she had made the move, already she could see the activities at the Manor where digging of the swimming pool and covered entrance had begun. 'Have they got planning permission or don't they need it?' she asked herself. 'Is it all part of the plot?'

She relaxed happily, the noise from the digger did not disturb her, it floated away into the distance. But suddenly it stopped and there seemed to be an atmosphere of unrest on the site. The foreman looked up, saw her and came hurriedly towards the 'Lodge'.

"Have you seen Dudley?" he shouted.

"He went off fairly early," answered Annie, "Can I be of any help?"

"We thought he'd know what to do," explained the man. "We've unearthed a body you see, and he is a Special."

An inner voice said to Annie, 'Don't get involved,' but it was no good, involvement followed Annie naturally.

15

"Leave it with me," she told him and went inside to try and phone Detective Inspector David. He was there. "It could be the missing six year old girl," she told him.

"Tell them to hold on, don't touch anything. I'll be right over."

He came. He was shortly due for retirement and a good 'case' was what he wanted. It might, with any luck, lead to promotion and leaving the force in a blaze of glory. Promotion might mean a higher pension. He was full of enthusiasm and motivation, the site soon became a hectic scene—the swimming pool forgotten.

The owner, Lance, had been fetched to find what he took to be the entire police force in occupation. It was some time before he realized that he was probably a suspect. But no, no, no, surely not?

"Troubles never come singly," Lance had said to her. "Did you hear that one of our neighbours has lost a little girl?"

"Lost?" asked Annie. "Lost could mean anything, even death."

"Kidnapped they think. She was playing in the garden. The police have been turned onto this now. As far as they know she's still alive, and bodies—well they'll still be bodies next week."

Thank God for Annie, but poor Annie, determined not to be involved, had shut her door and drawn her curtains. Bodies and kidnappings—No thank you!

Inspector David, grateful to Annie, visited her at teatime.

"Five bodies," he told her, "all lying higgledy-piggledy on top of each other, would you believe it. I've never seen anything like it. What do you make of that? Five, five, that's odd isn't it?"

They looked at each other. Yes it was odd.

"So it's not the small girl?" asked Annie.

"All grown up—no small girl," he answered.

They were referring to what the village spoke of as a kidnapping, last seen playing in the garden it was, at the moment, an overwhelming topic. Theories and accusations were on all lips.

She knew the story of the missing five (all grown up)

It was a London mystery with a world-wide following, everyone knew of the mysterious disappearance of 'THE FIVE'. There were no clues. They lived in a North London suburb and except for the fact that they all lodged in the same house, there was no connection between them. But all five, 3 men and 2 women, had disappeared on the same night leaving no trace whatsoever as to what could have happened or why. The media went to town on it.

CHAPTER 4

Five People

HILDA PALMER LOVED HER HOUSE, she and her sister Becky had been born there. Years back their parents had managed to buy it and now it was all hers. It was in North London and it suited her. The house had four bedrooms and two reception rooms. One of these was very small but the kitchen was big and Hilda mainly lived there. She had never married. Becky, christened Rebecca, had given up all rights to the house as it had been left to them jointly. She had gone to Australia and had written, "ME want a grubby old house in a mean street in filthy old London. No way. It's all yours and may it bring you luck." The solicitors on both sides had agreed that this was a signed document and now the house was Hilda's to do with what she wanted. She worked at the checkout in the nearest supermarket and was nearly due for retirement. She would take three nice lodgers, ladies—teachers perhaps—and she would then, after she retired, not have to penny-pinch.

At closing time she was about to put up her notice which said that 'This checkout is now closed' when a young man came up to her.

"How do I get a job here?" he asked her.

Odd, she thought and was about to suggest the Job Centre when looking at him, tidy, trim, washed but too thin she thought, he's somebody's son and just the sort I would have liked.

"I'm Mrs Palmer," she said, "Just go and mention my name at Customer Services."

Next day he was back. "Thank You," he said. "There was a job and with your recommendation I got it." Then he asked, "Do you know of some reasonable lodgings?"

"In for a penny, in for a pound," she thought as she handed over her address. She had one lodger. His name was **Gordon Barnes**, he had good references, the last from an old people's home where he had been a general dogs-body, now, in the supermarket, he was filling shelves.

One evening when she was tired and struggling down her road with shopping, Hilda saw a man going from door to door down the street. As he turned from a house he saw her, came towards her and said, "Let me carry those, they look heavy."

"The week's shopping, "she told him, "and yes, it is heavy."

"Do you live here?" he asked her.

"Three more doors down," she replied. She looked at him more closely. In his fifties perhaps, a comfortable type, balding a bit.

"Do you know of lodgings down here, I'm working on the new road, I'm a foreman new to the place, flats are expensive and I'm only temporary? Sheffield's my town."

They reached her door and she made a decision. "I've one lodger," she said. "Come in and meet him, he works in the supermarket and should be in?"

Gordon recognized a father figure and **Stan Butler**, for that was the newcomer's name, someone unlikely to cause trouble. They nodded, said, "Hiya mate," and accepted the new situation.

"I can take three," said Hilda, "so if you hear of anyone." What had happened to her lady teachers?

One evening, carrying a heavy tray, she slipped and fell heavily, she cried out and the men came running from the other room where they were watching football. They were most concerned.

"Seems to be broken," said Stan cheerfully, looking at her wrist.

"It could just be a sprain. Better get it x-rayed. I'll get the car." He kept his old banger in a small car park around the corner, "We'll go to A&E, back for supper. Better get it started. Oh, it's on the go, do watch it," he said to Gordon. Stan fetched his car and they helped a recovering Hilda into it, recovering from the shock but still in some pain. Gordon was watching supper.

It was all go at the hospital. It appeared to be some sort of changeover, the end of one shift and another coming on. Stan went in search of a wheelchair, he returned not only with a chair but a kind looking man pushing it. "What happed here?" he asked Hilda.

"I fell," she told him, she added, "Are you a doctor?"

He looked around a bit furtively and, trying to avoid Stan's eye. "I'm a nurse," he told her.

"An excellent profession, I'm sure." What was the matter with the man, what was wrong with being a nurse she asked herself?

"I wanted to be a doctor but—well—there wasn't the money."

They went down to X-ray, chatting comfortably.

"You can go home," they told her. "Nothing broken, just don't fall about."

"Where do you live?" Hilda asked the Nurse. She had already asked his name. He was **John Hedges**. "I mean do you live in?" Was this a silly question she asked herself?

"Sort of," he replied, "I wish I could find somewhere, do you know of anything?"

"You've got all my details," she replied. "I do have a room, if you're interested ring me."

They reached the outer doors and Stan was waiting. Hilda introduced them, they got her into the car and Stan drove off.

"Number three," he asked.

"Possibly," said Hilda. "We'll see."

John did ring and yes, he became No. 3.

Hilda retired, she had many friends. After doing her housework, deciding on supper, and shopping, she accepted invitations to coffee mornings or 'a cuppa' at almost any time of day. Her special friend who lived near was Emma Williams. Emma had a daughter in the police force and Hilda and Emma often laughed together about her exploits.

It was Gordon's birthday and supper was finishing with a special treat—his favourite—treacle pudding served with cream. There was a fat sort of silence as they ate.

A knock on the door broke the silence.

"See who it is," Hilda said. John rose and opened the door to a young girl who asked, "Is this a hotel or a home?"

"Better come in," John replied as if it answered the question—she was much too thin. Stan placed a chair for her, she eyed the pudding and Gordon served a generous portion, John poured the cream. She picked up a fork.

"You can't eat cream with a fork," said Gordon, handing her a spoon.

Silence reigned again. Hilda said nothing. Perhaps this odd scene would explain itself.

"I'm **Penny**," she said. "I'm at Uni and my group is doing a survey of this district, someone else is on traffic and parking and things. I'm finding out what goes on in all the houses. You'd be surprised," she added.

"I doubt it," said Hilda, "we've all grown up here."

"All one family?" questioned Penny.

"I hope you learn about people as well as houses," Hilda spoke stiffly, "Look again, how could we be?"

Penny did look, "You could have had three different husbands," she suggested.

"Put the kettle on MOTHER," John spoke with a laugh. Penny was a bit put-out. No-one had answered her questions but she was too full of pudding to argue.

"Where does that go?" she asked, pointing to the far door.

"It's our extra sitting room," replied Hilda. "The telly is in the other room," that explained it didn't it?

Penny got up and opened the far door, she gasped with pleasure, "It's perfect," she said.

"Well, of all the cheek," said Gordon.

Penny went into the room which contained little furniture. A very shabby sofa looking object, a table, chair and what could be a bookcase. "Perfect," she said again, she went over to the possible sofa and fiddled with it. It opened up into a bed.

"It's a put-u-up," she said.

Hilda, who had by now followed her in, said, "Well I never. I had no idea, I'm sure it was never used."

"Perhaps someone left it here," suggested Stan.

"I've a foam mattress that would fit it," said Penny hopefully, would you charge me much?"

"Not much if you give me a hand, I've sprained my wrist you see." Well why not thought Hilda, she seems a nice child and will be out of the way there.

They all looked at each other and laughed when Penny had gone with a cheery grin saying, "I'll get my things, I haven't much. I'll be back later."

"Birthday treat do you think," suggested Gordon. "Reminds me when you were talking money. I overhead a man talking in millions, I was behind the shelves, I shouldn't have heard, it was b . . . . y peculiar, part of some involved plot. Should I tell the police do you think?"

"Leave it, not your business," Stan considered the consequences—too much talk.

"Agreed, forget it," said Hilda, "It'll sort itself."

It did of course and one consequence mystified half the world for many years.

CHAPTER 5

ANNIE HAD OPENED THE DOOR reluctantly to Inspector David. She had told herself she would go away, she would definitely not get involved, but his wife and been good to her when she was in hospital (see Annie's Case Book). She was aware as she did so that she was involving herself and that was not what she had intended but she must now take the consequences. It was no good, she was now part of it.

"I do remember the five mystery but it was in London and very remote. Three years ago wasn't it or thereabouts. All five living in one house disappeared without trace, the media had, well, hardly a field day, it went on for weeks and it hasn't been forgotten?" Perhaps it has nothing to do with it."

"By no means," he answered her, "and now five bodies turn up in a remote spot miles away. Too much of a coincidence, but we shall soon know, there's plenty to go on now, the laboratories will have a field day. Also five together, if it had been one at a time—but five together—it's too much."

They were silent for a minute.

"Do you remember Sergeant Williams?" asked the Inspector. "It was thought a good idea to send her here for a first assessment. She'll be staying a few days. She knows both places, you see, and her mother was a friend of the missing landlady."

"Yes, we used to go swimming together, we shan't be doing much of that this time," Annie nodded towards the plot where the bodies had been found, I don't imagine that the pool idea will receive much enthusiasm."

The phone rang. It was Neil LaCoste. He was in a 'mood' as she put it. "It seems to me that you go out of your way to involve yourself in dangerous events. This could be dangerous! Why aren't you safely with a family watching over you in that sunny little bungalow?"

"It's for you," said Annie to Inspector David and handed over the phone. The Inspector stood up very straight and answered questions unheard by Annie.

"Yes Sir, certainly Sir, no Sir."

After putting the phone down he said, "It seems that the bodies' case is in some way connected to a case he is on, also in some way there is a child kidnapping. I know he works on people trafficking and this latest has him mad. You do remember him?"

"Oh yes," said Annie and, "When do I expect Sergeant Williams?"

"Any moment I expect, she's already on her way"

"I'd better go," he said to Annie.

As the Inspector left she added, "Give my love to your wife. Even with drama all around us we must keep up normality and decencies.

Tracy wasted no time, she arrived at Annie's cottage full of her 'case'. "Do you like it here," she asked Annie. "It's a bit of a change isn't it, after The Lilacs?"

"I did like it yes, with this wretched leg I couldn't do what I wanted in the garden. I've let it to Australians—they've promised . . ." she paused.

"It was fine here until . . ." she paused again, "We can hardly look forward to the swimming." Tracy agreed with this.

"I'm only here for a couple of days, why don't you come back with me, Mother won't mind."

Annie considered. Get away for all this trouble—well why not? Before this devastating discovery and depressing discussion, this delving into the past, she had been full of Sally's wedding for she and Bob had decided to get married. Mother of the bride must have a new outfit and this included a new bra. Oh! Yes, an excellent place London, there was even somewhere that actually fitted that necessary garment.

"Could you spare the time to come shopping with me?" she asked Tracy.

"How are you on the back of a motorbike?" Tracy now asked hopefully.

"You're impossible," Annie told her. "By the way, where are you staying?"

"At the village pub, it's a bit . . . it isn't for long."

"Move in here and we'll be off when you're ready. No to the motorbike, I'll drive to the station, leave the car there and pick it up on the way back."

A moment's thought. "I rather fancy blue, what do you think?"

Her mind was a long way from mysterious, tragic puzzles and old Alf's enjoyment of them.

Tracy moved in, she regretted the swimming pool but, Annie thought, that aspect was for the pleasure she and Annie would have had together, deck chairs, cool drinks, she did not at any time harp upon abandoned bodies. Perhaps a good thing, Annie thought, if she was to make an objective report. Her attitude towards the village inhabitants was very different. They were a 'surly' lot. Who did they think she was, conversation ceased when she appeared. She had offered drinks (she had been told to be generous) but no-one ever accepted or offered one in return. The food was awful and background music not at all 'background'. As to the Post Office—she had never met such insolence—she had a good mind to report it!

Annie, her mind on Sally's wedding, said, "Poor old Tracy," she added, "I am looking forward to London."

Annie was well aware that Tracy had the wrong attitude, approach or feelings to a village that felt itself in mourning. They had lost a beloved child and in no way was a self-centered busy-body Sergeant any consolation. They had been promised a Superintendent and nothing less would do.

They also had a mysterious creepy and equally unpopular stranger staying in the village. Someone thought he was the Post Mistress's Toy Boy so he was known as this, but Mrs Hughes denied all knowledge of him.

Miranda Foster was a favourite and of much greater importance if she was still alive than five unknown bodies. Even the Vicar—a worthy woman—had agreed to this.

(When Annie heard the tale and later met the village she thought that she had not dared to do anything else)

CHAPTER 6

ANNIE SAID "NO" VERY FIRMLY to the idea of going up to London with Tracy on the back of the motorbike. She travelled up by train, leaving her car at the station. In spite of the no motorbike plea, Tracy was at the London station to meet her. "What the Hell", Annie said to herself as Tracy led her to it, the station was crowded and it was hot. So in a determined manner Annie swung her good leg over and clung on tightly.

"Mother is looking forward to meeting you," Tracy told her.

"Why?" asked Annie suspiciously.

"I've told her all about the things you do and how well we get on together."

Annie accepted this and hoped that the stories hadn't been exaggerated. She was still suspicious when she met Mrs Williams. Mrs W gushed, everything she did was in capital letters. "Call me Betty—everybody does."

"Did Tracy show you the house? I'll see the Griffiths, that's the name of the tenants, and we'll go over it! You'll like that I'm sure. I've done up the spare room for you. Is that all the luggage you've got?"

She paused and Annie said "Tracy did point out a house, I wasn't thinking . . ."

"Take Mrs Butcher's luggage up Tracy, I'll put the kettle on," said Betty.

Annie was almost immediately annoyed, she had a useful knapsack, she was going shopping, she had all she needed, she had no intention of getting involved in Tracy's 'case' or in houses of murder. She smiled as sweetly as possible and allowed Tracy to show her to her room.

Tracy said, "We'll do all that she's planned for us and get it off our backs. "Then," she paused, "We can go shopping and do our own thing. Okay by you?"

Annie bowed to the inevitable, she was tired and London was all hustle and bustle. Now for a quiet supper, television and bed. Tomorrow she would allow herself to be talked at, to see the places Mrs Williams had planned, after which she would be free to follow her own pursuits. She felt guilty though. She was a guest and was using this opportunity to look at London shops.

"I've seen the Griffiths," said Betty next morning. "We'll go over after breakfast, it's only just round the corner, they've lots to show you. The media have picked the case up again, you see, and everyone is interested again. At the time they helped to do a real 'tour', they knew Hilda, it was a very exciting time."

Annie had not realized that Tracy's home was so near to the 'Mystery Five' house, had she not been listening? Perhaps not. She had not the slightest intention of being part of any 'tour' whatever that might involve and had they to put up with Betty's presentation of the events. She glanced at Tracy who said, "Mum, you've got a dentist appointment don't forget."

"Have I?"

"Yes, of course you have," replied Tracy who had made it herself only half an hour ago, stressing the urgency of the case.

"We had better see the Griffiths and hear local gossip but at least we shan't have Mum's version as well," explained Tracy without guilt. "The trouble is," she went on, "that you are at the other end, didn't you discover the bodies? Even if you didn't everyone thinks you did."

Annie resigned herself to the situation, if nothing else she would take some information back to her friend, Inspector David.

The new tenants, the Griffiths, were pleased to live in a house of notoriety, they were disappointed that time had lessened the interest, they were still ready to talk about it. They had collected a small party of friends and neighbours to meet Annie. "We did a lot to the house, it had been a well-kept place when the old lady (well not so very old) and her lodgers were here. The police took the place apart, dug up the cellar floor, made holes in the walls, there was nothing left. All I rescued were a few recipe books (I was looking for a different Christmas pudding recipe). The police flicked through them, said there was nothing there, nothing of interest to them, I mean, there were plenty of Christmas Party ideas," she finished with a laugh. She showed them the books.

Annie took the proffered pile, she sat and with her usual deliberation started to go through them.

She held up an old letter, "They left this?" she asked.

"The police seemed to think it had nothing to do with the case."

Annie returned it to the recipe collection. "Why am I considered to be part of this, what have I done to deserve this?" thought Annie. I came here under the misapprehension that I was getting away from it. Because I knew Tracy in different circumstances and, let's face it, because I was amused by her clumsy but well-meaning progress; or has she been very clever and used me. I was known to have been there when the Mysterious Five were discovered but no more. There has been no mention of identification. As far as Annie knew it was still speculation but here she was expected to give and to know all the ins and outs of the business. Annie was angry with herself and not only because she was being shown off as part of the 'tour' but because she had a sudden burst of interest—here were clues and, whether she liked it or not, they were in her hands. She had an audience but in no way was going to show her inner interest. A neighbour, anxious not to be missed out, said, "I took the cat."

Annie clung to this—a way out perhaps. Aloud she said, "Of all the stories I've ever heard there was no mention of a cat."

"Perhaps the police held it for questioning," suggested another neighbour. The laughter gave Annie a short breathing space.

"How-do-I-get-out-of-this" was occupying her mind when she was jerked back into the scene of the moment.

"We often fed the cat."

"I always said I'd take the cat. We weren't sure what was going on, you see?"

"It's a very friendly animal."

"It's the cat she fell over when she sprained her wrist, she didn't see it and she was . . ." the words faded in Annie's mind and only the strange click she occasionally felt when there was a piece of jigsaw that should fit.

This was the first time a sprained wrist had been mentioned and in some way that so far she did not know, it was important.

The tenant was again explaining about the only souvenirs she had managed to rescue. "I was looking for a different Christmas Pudding recipe."

Annie was enthusiastic as she still held the pile of recipes, oddments of news, letters and grubby coloured leaflets all tucked into an old recipe book. The police had dismissed it as unimportant, and about the Methodists. Annie would make her own decisions. It certainly didn't look like evidence in a worldwide 'Mystery Fives' murder case.

"That's JUST what I want, some new Christmas ideas, especially a pudding."

If her audience were disappointed they didn't say so, coffee was offered, a new supermarket discussed and Tracy managed to excuse them, "I must pick up poor Mother from the dentist."

But Annie was homesick or so she told herself. Plenty of people were using mobiles so there must be a good signal here. She looked round for Tracy who was very busy, she'd gone into a shop to try something on. Annie rang Maggie, "Could you have a crisis, definitely needing my presence?"

"Whatever you say," replied Maggie, understanding.

"And could you demand my return at about supper time tonight on the house number I gave you?"

"Without a doubt," (more understanding).

The phone rang during supper. Tracy answered it. "It's Mrs Hurst," she told Annie, "she needs to speak to you, she sounds very upset."

Regretting the subterfuge Annie spoke in a soothing voice, "Of course I'll come, don't worry, yes, yes it's okay, my car is at the station," she rang off. She now looked at a list on the wall headed 'Useful Numbers'. There was a taxi number there so she ordered one for the morning, she then returned to her anxious hosts to apologize for her unexpected call and need to return.

"Shopping, yes, it's sad but after all there are very good High Street shops back home."

She departed next morning with many regrets and an invitation to Tracy to stay at the cottage if she was sent to the other end of the mystery once more.

Annie still had the so-called Recipe Book and its odd contents. She was going to show it to her friend Inspector David.

Hopefully Inspector David would see a larger pension if upgraded. Anxious that the 'case' should stay his 'case' and Annie never interferes—just helps one to think so, yes, a nice chat with Mrs B.

It was an enlightening talk and they were both satisfied with it.

Annie saw the light whilst talking to him, "I should have seen it," she was excited.

"Seen what?" he asked hopefully.

"The wrist, someone else wrote it, the young lodger who worked in a care home was the Methodist, he wouldn't bend the rules."

It took Inspector David a few minutes to digest this but when it came—"That letter?" he questioned.

"Exactly, they missed it—you've found the answer." He loved the 'you'.

He took the letter saying, "How I came by it is nobody else's business." They laughed like conspirators.

"Thank you," he said as he left.

CHAPTER 7

NEIL WAS WAITING FOR HER as she arrived at her cottage. He had managed to work himself up into a good fury.

"What do you think you're playing at? These are vile, dangerous people, this is no play-acting. You are not only in the middle of the 'Mystery Five' body Inquiry but you go off to London to investigate the other end. You are now a marked woman. People who will arrange the complete disappearance of five people, without clues may I remind you, will think nothing of the quiet disappearance of an interfering female living alone in a remote spot." He was practically speechless, "and now here you are again waiting for trouble. We are dealing with an organization that seems to have endless connections, mostly evil and its finances are limitless." He paused for breath and Annie was ready for him.

"Neil," she protested, "it is no use being angry with me or blaming me for being in places at the wrong time. I am not, repeat not, involved in any way. I did not break my leg on purpose and you started grumbling at me then. I could no longer manage my garden and came here at the express wish of Lance and Maggie. They had no idea that they had bodies in the area designated for a swimming pool. I rang Inspector David because I know him and thought he was the best person to deal with the situation. I suppose you are staying with Dudley and Rose and have already heard all the local gossip and 'some'."

Annie went on to tell him as briefly as possible of events in London. She did not tell him of her removal of possible clues which she intended for Inspector David.

She continued, "I shall not enquire into who, in their wisdom, sent Sergeant Williams to stay in a village where she was met with a stony silence because that is the effect she has. What was needed was a quiet listener not a full blooded brass-hatted major-general. There must be a niche in the force for such as her. We made friends in a swimming pool and I thought nothing of her invitation. No-one told me that she and her mother lived practically next door to the mystery house. I was glad to get away from the hullaballoo here and my mind was on shopping for an outfit to wear for my daughter's wedding. I came away as soon as I could and that had nothing to do with crime unless you consider my underhand method of achieving it, for I got Maggie to ring me and say there was a crisis in school. Sorry Neil, if I let personal feelings get in the way of a good investigation but the truth is I couldn't stand Mrs Williams and I wasn't in a mood to try."

Neil acknowledged her truthful outburst and in a calmer way replied, "We shall never know what threw this group of five into the path of this particularly loathsome scheming gang. They knew something, you may know something. People trafficking is bad enough, little girls for the sex trade is surely the lowest of the low."

"I'm not a little girl Neil. I can look after myself."

"So, I am sure, could five grownups. Your story," he went on, "is a peculiar mixture, cats, swimming pools, shopping and I caught a hint of recipes. There seemed a great jumble of events and you are jumbling it even further and come out with . . ."

"A very clever deduction I am sure you were going to say, "Annie interrupted him innocently. "As you know I'm a teacher and have never pretended to be anything else."

He laughed, "Tell me, please, in words of one syllable, how you have managed to set all the tongues wagging, to cheer Inspector David, to quieten Sergeant Williams, to upset Rose Russell for a start. I'll have a guard put on this place."

"I'd rather you didn't, if that doesn't set tongues wagging I'd be interested to know what would." She sat down. "Put the kettle on," she said. "We'll part friends."

Annie rang the Inspector again when Neil had gone. "Can you bring the police records of 'the five'. I knew a bit about them once but need to refresh my memory. I know I thought the police concentrated on the wrong one but why I thought this I can't remember." What am I doing she thought.

"I'll be right over," he agreed.

He came and handed over the following:

1. Hilda Palmer home owner—just retired from supermarket, worked on tills.
2. Penny Higgins—student at LSE, London University. Parents devastated, eldest of three.
3. Gordon Barnes—worked in supermarket, recommended by Mrs Palmer so taken on. Little known about him. Parents gone away very upset, spoilt later son perhaps. Colleagues said a Methodist.
4. Stan Butler—the one the police concentrated on. Wife now moved to Liverpool and remarried. Annoyed at reopening of case.
5. John Hedges—nurse—no relations, was hoping to emigrate.

These were his notes. "But", he said, "it is them, DNA and all the tests including dental. Now what?"

Annie wasn't sure. One thing she was sure about, she wasn't going to be told what to do and to have a police guard hanging about. How dare Neil dictate to her.

The notes were a bit sketchy—much shortened. The police had spent weeks on interviews with family, friends and fellow workers all to no avail. The case had remained open with little hope of it being solved until now. Now, however wasn't bring much new light, but it was news again.

Annie knew students when she saw them. They were the right age, slightly scruffy but not outrageously so. They were typical of the sixth form leavers not quite sure of the next move. She could soon think up suitable questions. What were your main subjects? Was this your main interest? Where did you want to go? Did you want to be near home or a long way away?

"Can I help you?" she asked.

"Are you Mrs Butcher?" The young man was to be spokesman. So they knew her name, she replied that she was, trying not to be too helpful. What was this?

The girl spoke, "We're Penny's brother and sister. I'm Frankie and this is my brother Doug. Mum and Dad didn't expect to go through all this again. We can have a funeral now as they say it is Penny, or what's left of her."

"We'd begun to forget. It's Frances really. How do we arrange a funeral?"

"There's Becky too," put in Doug. "Someone told us about you."

"Told you what about me?" Annie was suspicious.

"How you help people and how you would be bound to be here," Frankie told her, "and here you are." It was simple to them.

"I don't see how I can help, I'm not in holy orders. And who is Becky?"

"Becky wants a funeral too. We knew you can't do it personally but we thought you'd know who would. To help the parents you see."

"Why me?" thought Annie, aloud she said, "I thought the sister was in Australia?"

"She's come over now that there are bodies, you can't have a proper burial if there's nothing to bury. She seems very lost and lonely, she doesn't like it over here."

Doug thought that funny and Frankie said, "It's probably more dangerous than being lost in the bush."

"Can we bring her to see you?" asked Doug, "She's upsetting the parents."

Annie agreed to this while inwardly and in horror pondering on having to arrange and attend five funerals.

"If I have said I'd do it I'd better get on with it," said Annie to herself as she drank her first cup of the morning whilst contemplating the early morning sun.

She decided to walk into the village, the exercise would do her leg good, it was almost back to normal and she had a stick.

She decided to visit the church first as this was in the centre of things, it had a pleasing and welcoming aspect and would provide local information. An attractive woman of about her own age appeared with a welcoming smile. She was wearing the usual ecclesiastical collar (a dog collar as Annie thought of it). Annie had not expected a woman Vicar, 'How stupid of me, there are plenty of woman vicars these days,' it was just that she had expected an 'oh-dear I-don't-think-I-can' sort of elderly man. This was so different.

Annie explained her mission. "I'm Janet," said the Vicar enthusiastically. "Bury all in one service. I'm sure we've room over there by the wall."

This couldn't be better thought Annie, "But I think one of them is a Methodist."

"No problem, I'll see Mr Anderson, he comes regularly, glad of an opportunity for a joint service to show how united we are. Great!" she finished, "We'll fix a date."

Annie couldn't thank her enough and promised some notes on which to base a suitable tribute.

"Now go and have coffee at our small café," said Janet. "Everything is homemade and lovely coffee. I'll try and join you when I've seen the flower arrangers."

A man could be seen leaving the Post Office. Annie thought that she had seen him before and he had not left a pleasant impression.

"I know what you mean," said Janet, although nothing had been said. "They call him Mrs Humphrey's Toy Boy—most unsuitable. She does B&B and he's been hanging around."

"I see," said Annie, but what did she see—she wasn't quite sure. "It seems extremely unlikely," she had already met up with the Post Mistress.

"Oh! Yes, most unlikely, but it gives a purpose to his presence. He tries, you see, to be mysterious and suggest secret police. But you would know if this were true," she added confidently.

Annie let this pass and did not question the source of any gossip for a Vicar would naturally hear all the talk.

"You knew about our former tragedy didn't you?" continued the Vicar. The mysterious five has completely wiped out all memory of it. No, I'm wrong, of course it hasn't to the family whose tragedy it was. The Fosters who live in that big brick house just outside the village. Miranda was playing in the garden, quite safe they thought, just disappeared. Everyone was appalled.

"I remember it well. This new business may awaken interest though or, as you say, may divert the media's attention."

"We'll see," said Janet.

Annie was greeted by a smile in the Post Office. "Don't do B&B at the Manor do they?" asked the good lady there. "I'm like to get rid of mine."

"Don't blame you," replied Annie, "but no."

She had coffee in the café and was enjoying a homemade cake when the Vicar joined her once more. Several other ladies joined them on seeing the Vicar and hoping to get the church's view on recent happenings. No gossip of course, not if the Vicar was there.

Annie left them to it. She was sure that the various topics would get full measure, she was also sure of another relieving headache, she would not have to go to five funerals, already the vicar would mentally have the whole business in hand.

The village was a pleasant one and a large archway led her into a well kept stable yard, and here was her Vicar! Well, no, but this comfortable late middle-aged and graying man was the person she had thought to see conducting a service in the church.

"Hello Miss," said this character, "I thought you'd find me—that is if you were the person I thought you were."

"Who did you think I was?" asked Annie.

"Why that private detective of course, everyone knows that. Call me Jock, everybody does."

"Jock? Short for?"

"Jockey—never lost a race. So you're okay now you've got me on the case. Do you want a bit of haunting?"

Annie laughed. "So you know all about that do you?" she asked.

"It kept the old man happy—no snoopers you understand. An innocent piano playing all night. It kept the young man at his practice. Didn't always have to be there—had gadgets fixed up, no fool that one, and inherited the house—worth something, that place." He paused for breath.

"Um-hum, (and again) Um-hum," said Annie after some thought. "I rather thought so."

"And an occasional midnight horse riding up there," continued Jock. "The listeners, weren't they 'knocking on the midnight door'? Learnt something like that at school."

Annie interrupted, "I'm surprised then, that a very dubious helicopter didn't alert him."

"I'm sure it did but everybody by then was suspicious, he'd gone too far and even the young one was talking of Old Peoples' Homes or worse."

Annie was intrigued—Lance, Lance, she said to herself, always knowing more than you should. Aloud she said, "Did you believe the chopper story?"

"I would, you know, if the price was right. You be careful of that 'Toy Boy'—nasty bit of work there."

Annie agreed, she saw the so-called 'Toy Boy' in the distance as she came out of the stable yard. What was he up to?

She left the village and went to the Manor. Dudley had been a bit mysterious and she hoped to catch him in his barn.

"Rose wants to see you," he'd said and then added, "Australians aren't too happy. Have a talk with Rose."

But why, Rose surely wasn't going to Australia. Rose didn't need to be mysterious, they had been friends long enough to discuss anything in an open manner. Dud was in his barn and Annie said she'd be in touch.

"Tell Rose I'll be over," she said reassuringly, but Dud, too, was worried and this disturbed Annie.

She joined the family for supper and promised Sam that she would take him to feed the ducks in the park 'at home' as he put it. But why? Why 'back home' and why a wish to feed ducks?

It was a lovely evening and it was not far to her cottage, an owl hooted, suddenly she felt a danger signal, an animal instinct of alarm. She tried the door but it was still locked, what was it? All was peaceful outside, she felt sure that someone not friendly towards her was there. How had he got in?

He was waiting for her and she was ready for him. He lifted the metal bar he was holding, an old-fashioned poker, part of the cottage furnishings she later found out. She dived low and threw him forward over her back. 'Did they teach me this in the Girl Guides?' she thought as she caught the poker, the door slammed behind her and he hit his head on the corner of a cupboard in the small hall as he came down, she hit him with the poker and sat on his head.

He appeared to be unconscious but she wasn't sure. Rather him than me. "Poor old Toy Boy," she said to him, as the door burst open and the whole police force seemed to be there, Neil leading them. All hell broke loose.

"Now do you believe me?" he shouted at her and pressed her comfortingly to him. She smelled the roughness and pleasure of his jacket, she returned his pressure and kiss."

"We're going to the hospital," he told her as an ambulance drew up.

"Is that for me or him," Annie asked.

"There's a car for you, Sir," said a constable, "And an escort."

"I live here," Annie pointed out, "I don't need the hospital."

"Clare and Rose are waiting for you," Dudley said now as he joined them, don't keep them waiting too long, they're like the proverbial cats on hot bricks."

"Where's Toy Boy going," Annie was worried, she didn't often use pokers in this way—a good heavy one too, she'd not noticed it before.

"We need him, he'll be well looked after."

"For interrogation?" asked Annie doubtfully.

"For questioning," he replied, "And before his so called friends get to him, they don't tolerate weak links as you know."

They got in the car.

"Is this a good time to ask you to marry me?" Neil was hesitant.

"No, for if he dies I'll be suspected of murder and your wife must be above suspicion," she answered. "I might hit you."

"I'd rather have you in a hitting mood than anyone else who didn't hit!"

"It's still 'No' at the moment Neil, but . . ."

"I shan't give up, I assure you."

"Oh good," she said as she snuggled up to him.

The old hospital to which they now drove (See Annie's Case Book) was almost unrecognizable in its quiet clean efficiency. It was now due for closure, it had had its day. Clare had been too good at hers.

"I've made that little room next to my office ready for you," she told Annie.

"Not your old room with bad memories," put in Rose.

"And now the best place in which to brick me up," complained Annie. "You planned to have me murdered, then I'm kidnapped. What's wrong with a bit of suffocation?"

The small ex-storeroom was a bit crowded but the Nigerian porter was told he wasn't needed. "Friends are always needed," he said, not quite sure of the present proceedings.

"I declare this meeting open," said Rose firmly.

"May I know what it's all about?" asked Annie, "And where is our friend John Watson, last time I was here . . ."

"He's at the Manor, making them an offer," interrupted Clare in her usual confident manner.

"You can't be serious, whoever would want such a place and now . . . I ask you?" Annie gasped.

"Do you want to stay there," Rose asked her.

"Rose, I've let my bungalow, they're there for at least a year."

"They're fed up with this country, want the unrestricted feel of the bush, longing for what they call home—so there you have it, you can go back to where you belong."

"But—the Manor?"

"We're going to make it into an Old Peoples' Home," explained Clare, "I shall run it."

"It will cost a fortune to make it habitable for the elderly."

"Yes," said Clare firmly and happily.

"Will the Hursts accept the offer?" asked Annie.

"I've no doubt of it," returned Clare.

"There's something else isn't there?" Annie knew that odd feeling of expectation. "Don't keep me in suspense."

Clare now interrupted, "Of course we should all welcome Rose and Victoria at the Manor for Rose's job here finishes as well as mine but she has other ideas."

"It's time you gave up this 'I'm not a detective, I'm a teacher' theme—well business. You know you're a detective and so does everyone else. 'Private Investigator' sounds better," said Rose.

"No it doesn't," said Annie, "How about The Annie Butcher C? Detective Agency? Can anyone think of a suitable C.? Perhaps at the next staff meeting they'll all have ideas?

"And I shall be what? We shall need a new computer, better let me choose that." Rose was already mentally sitting behind it.

"You're very welcome, you shall be Assistant, but please don't forget who is The Boss of this new establishment.

❧❦

THE ABC
DETECTIVE AGENCY

Joy Reid

The A B **C**

C? careful
Capable
Colossal
Civilised
charming
creative?
companionable
complete
Commendable.

Detective Agency

Proprietor Annie Butcher
~~Secretary~~? Rose Russell..
Assistant
No ~~applications~~ turned away.
client ~~? MS~~

CHAPTER 1

WITH A SHOCK ANNIE HAS changed her mind. Yes, she is a detective, why deny it? She might have to go on teaching, perhaps to an evening class on 'The difficulties of the Amateur Detective' and later 'My More Exciting Cases'. She hoped that some would be exciting, but now she could pick and choose, for the moment anyway. She hoped that finance wouldn't be too big a trouble.

There was great astonishment at the next staff meeting of The George Pound School when Maggie told everyone that Mrs Butcher had resigned. "Fortunately we now have Mr Sleep (Dan Sleep) who will take over her non-teaching duties as well as her classes, he has been officially appointed as Deputy Head."

Dan rose and acknowledged this introduction.

"It's disgraceful," said Caroline Boots, "Not telling us and . . ."

"She has let me know Caroline, and I'm telling you so stop fussing." Always Caroline, thought Maggie.

"It sounds interesting, not to say exciting," put in Alison in a hopeful sort of voice.

"Et tu Alison," retorted Maggie, "Please NO."

Alison replied, "Not yet anyway, we'll see how it works out."

Caroline intervened again, "You'll see, for financially it will be a disaster. I like a monthly cheque myself."

"She has Rose Russell with her, she runs the finances and business side of the old hospital. She's very good I've heard and the hospital is being closed down. Annie is living up there at the moment."

"Is that where she is?" said another member of staff. There were Australians in her bungalow when I called. Was that attack part of being a detective?"

"There you are, you see," Caroline again. "She'll soon give it up."

Before there was further discussion on Annie's domestic arrangements Maggie said, "Any Other Business," waited a moment and said, "I declare this meeting closed," before Caroline could once more bring up her own views. Alison's reassuring presence had to satisfy her.

Annie was still living at the hospital. No longer in a stuffy store room, she and Clare had smartened up what had probably been a night nurse's 'hideout' or somewhere convenient and essential for their duties. There was a small kitchen and two other rooms, she used one as a bedroom and the other (with bits and pieces found by Clare or Dudley) as a sitting room or office. There was also a washroom with shower. She felt secure here but hoped to get back to her bungalow when the Australians had gone and the 'Toy Boy' excitement had died down.

"This would suit us perfectly," said Rose.

"I suppose it would, a perfect situation I admit, but we have no idea what the NHS intend to do with it."

"We could buy the lot and let it off as flats or offices," suggested Rose.

"Now don't let's get above ourselves," returned Annie. "I have no intention of going into high finance. I do agree that as an office site it would be ideal. Why don't you look into it?"

"I will. It's a perfect position, discreet but semi-central, an interview room for you and this bigger room for all my equipment and records."

"Perhaps John Watson will buy it?" But John Watson was too busy with his Old Peoples' Home. Eventually a big building firm bought the hospital and was surprised at the excellent condition of the building. Flats and offices were to be its fate and the one tenant already in possession was very welcome and gave a good tone to the place.

The Australians moved from Annie's bungalow 'The Lilacs' and a good office routine was started at the 'ABC Detective Agency'.

"It's not quite Baker Street," said Annie, "but we shall make a good start here." She was surprised at how much she missed the hustle and bustle of school. Not so much the order and regularity but for the pupils themselves, their characters, their troubles, difficulties and successes. She was pleased when Linda Green, a sixth-former walked nervously into her office.

"Linda, how nice to see you, not the hospital I hope?"

"I'm pregnant," said Linda.

Annie was about to be a bit flippant but stopped herself from saying 'It's the maternity ward you want!' Instead she said, "Sit down Linda—talk to me." Linda sat.

Maggie had said nothing about Linda. She had, however, mentioned the Martins who had left unexpectedly and leaving everything behind them. Maggie half suggested that Annie would find out why. Now here was Liz Martin's 'best friend', she might possibly know what happened. To find out with no trouble to herself might impress Maggie and create a good image.

"You must miss Liz Martin, did she know of your trouble?"

"Oh yes. It was him you see, her Dad. We were all drunk, horribly so—it was horrid but when I told them they were *horrider* still and Liz's Mum walked out and went to her people in Norwich. It's a long way off. Nobody need know need they?" Linda was crying now and obviously deeply distressed.

Annie could think of nothing to say. She tried a few soothing words and put her arm round Linda. She thought, 'what a very peculiar mixture the Detective Agency is going to be. I could charge the school for finding out where the Martins are but on the other hand I most certainly couldn't tell this depressing tale. And a baby, so many wanted them (how much for a baby) and then so many didn't. Where do I come in?'

Aloud she said, "Tell me what you want to do Linda. You're not alone now so no worries." It sounded okay.

Linda says, "Liz's Mum and Dad have made it up now. Dick (that's Liz's Dad) has given up drink and he's got a job in Norwich. Liz's Mum says she'll adopt it. My Mum's furious."

"It's no use being furious after the event," said Annie, "but all is well, you can come and live with me at 'The Lilacs' until you've had it. We can do some study and you can go back to school when it's all over. People will talk but who cares, you've 'Uni' to look forward to and you don't drink—okay?"

Linda went on crying, from happiness she explained.

I need company at 'The Lilacs' Annie told herself. I'll get her all A*s and this will be behind her. Perhaps this will satisfy Neil who said he'd rather she stayed where she was. Maybe he would but this seemed the ideal solution and he was on the other side of the world chasing evil do-ers.

It was sad that baby's stay would be such a short one but Joel's affair seemed fairly solid and Sally and Bob had decided on a full blooded wedding with Hog Roast after the ceremony. Good for them.

John Watson, having made sure that Clare would run '**The Manor Residential Home for the Elderly**' now asked her to marry him and was accepted, they seemed to be inviting everybody.

Annie's mind was on what to wear. She consulted Rose but this was unproductive, Rose had plenty to wear thank you very much but, "I will come shopping with you." Rose loved shopping whilst Annie only shopped if there was no alternative.

"Would the same outfit do for both weddings?" she asked Rose hopefully.

"Certainly not!" replied Rose, "Mother of the Bride needs a bit of a splash out whereas the friend you helped to . . ."

"They needed no help," Annie interrupted.

Rose continued, "As I was saying—fairly new friends of a certain age, you need a more mature look. We shall enjoy looking around."

Annie was not so confident but Rose had been invited to both weddings and would in all probability be finding something she must have.

"Mature? Good idea," said Annie, thinking, 'I'll base myself on the Queen—she has a top-quality mature look. Rose's idea of a bit of a splash and mine may differ and Sally will not be bothering about how I look. She will look splendid.'

CHAPTER 2

I T WAS A TIME OF change and movement so it was not surprising that young Sam was disturbed. There was so much talk, a lot of which had gone over his head. Certain images stuck and worried him. 'Australia? They weren't going there were they?' He thought of his real home and not a great rambling house with endless police and bodies. The piano was great but Dad said it was his and they'd put in somewhere, but where? Home to Sam was the well run, well organized village on the outskirts of town. The beautifully planted park was nearby. He went to see Annie.

"Park? Feed the ducks there, we can go anytime—now if you like. What have you got in the way of feeding material?"

He disappeared and returned shortly with a large bag which he said were 'crusts'. Annie accepted the word and found her own bag of crusts. They went to the park. Annie not only knew the only gardener they could see, but the car park attendant. She had taught his son who was now doing well. This appreciative father now found a good space for Annie and Sam. They went in search of ducks.

They were not the only visitors. There was a large party of children, they were in the charge of a couple of rather grim-looking women. Is this a local school, funny or fishy, it bothered Annie? I'm a detective and if I want to be bothered I shall be. Sam was only interested in the ducks.

"That's a pretty one," he was trying to get Annie's attention.

Yes, there was a pretty one, a very pretty one and also pretty miserable looking. Sam was looking at ducks, Annie at the children.

"Sam," she said, "do you see those children, could you sort of drift towards them and mix with them a bit."

He sighed, "They're all girls," he complained.

All girls—how extraordinary, a girls' school. No there couldn't be, she was on her home ground, she would know of it. This was a hasty unexpected stop or break, perhaps one of them was sick? She looked again, that pretty one had been in the news, how long ago, just long enough for the faded memory to remain.

"Sam, just do as I say, don't question it."

"Right Boss," he said, getting the feel of adventure.

"Go to that one in the blue dress, the pretty one, take her hand and say 'RUN' and run. Run to the car park attendant. I'll be there." Sam nodded.

"NOW"

Sam ran, the little girl ran with him. Annie pretended she wasn't involved, she was good at this, knowing a different way to the car park she used this and joined the others by the car.

"Get going," said the attendant. "The nearest Police Station is in Park Street—a missing girl, aren't you wonderful!"

Teaching had been useful, she knew so many parents, she remembered his boy but didn't stay for a chat. She drove to Park Street and they entered the station. A bored policeman greeted them. "Yes, is it important?"

"I think so," said Annie, "and this is Miranda," she paused, "Do you know your other name?" she asked.

Don't even know your names?" he laughed, "What do you expect me to do?" He laughed again, "don't tell me, you're the famous Annie Butcher?"

"Yes," said Annie as another policeman came in from behind the desk. "Mrs Butcher" he said with surprise and respect. "What has happened?"

"She says . . . do you mean she really is?" Confusion overcame the policeman on desk duty. His chance for fame and he'd lost it.

The recent arrival took over firmly. "It's Miranda Foster isn't it? Trust you, I'll ring the parents. Do you know your phone number?" he asked Miranda.

She did, "I know my numbers," she told Annie.

The policeman rang the number and handed the phone to Miranda, "Mummy," she said. There was a nasty bump at the other end. Miranda looked puzzled. A man's voice came on, "Who is it?"

"Daddy," said Miranda—another nasty bump.

The Sergeant arrived, "You seem to be particularly inept," he said to the duty policeman. He spoke loudly into the phone. "Is that you Madam, we have Mrs Butcher and a young assistant here at the police station."

There was a voice now at the other end, "Is Annie Butcher there herself?"

"Yes Madam, and I suggest you come as fast as you can."

"Humphrey! Humphrey!" said the voice, "Get the car quickly."

Humphrey didn't sound fit to drive but the phone went dead and the Sergeant said, "Will someone put the kettle on. Can someone fetch something nice for the young man, ice cream perhaps?"

"Could you make it two?" asked Miranda.

"Surely," agreed the young policeman, leaving hastily. First with the news—would you believe it!

They were enjoying the ice creams when Miranda's parents arrived. It was an emotional scene. Annie hoped that all her cases would end so satisfactorily. She and Sam drove home.

"Nice kid," he said. "Do assistants always get ice creams?"

"Always," said Annie.

CHAPTER 3

The Case of the Lost TEDDY BEAR

A TEARFUL VOICE ON THE phone said, "My little girl has lost her Teddy Bear. You say no case is too small. Do you do Teddy Bears? Maybe on a bus."

On a bus? Annie's heart sank, had it come to lost toys. Aloud she said cheerfully, "Teddy Bears, of course, regularly, why what happened?"

"My husband has just died, he had Malaria. My little Sylvia has lost her dear Daddy, and now, (sob) her Teddy Bear." Which matters most, Daddy or Teddy?

"Come and see me as soon as you can. I'll see what I can do," replied Annie.

For, on Annie's desk, was sitting a benign looking Teddy, it appeared to smile at her. His was a vey different story ~

A very well dressed affluent middle-aged woman had dumped a plastic bag on Annie's desk. My grand-daughter found this, she took a fancy to it but we don't believe in 'finders keepers' so could you find a home for it. My husband and I are off to the Bahamas. My daughter is getting a divorce from the waste-of-space man she married. Lily my grand-daughter is going to her father's. We've bought her a new one—Teddy Bear not father. HE would probably have let her keep it. I haven't washed it. There it is." She nodded at the plastic bag and departed. Annie watched her advance towards a flashy car.

To the plastic bag she said, "Hello old chap. Have you come to stay?"

It hadn't of course, for about teatime a sad looking girl (not much more thought Annie) with a smaller edition of herself who rushed to the desk with cries of delight. "Teddy!" she gathered him up. "Oh! Thank you."

She had good manners. Annie said, "Let's put the kettle on."

Rose came through the door to join the party, she contributed in the form of some very good biscuits meant for Dudley.

There was a knock on the outer door and a very nervous young man entered. He held the hand of another small girl also clutching a Teddy Bear, a new one. She hopefully eyed the biscuits.

"Join the party," said Rose.

"You ought to have a bell," said the young man.

"Do you do bells?" Annie asked him.

"I sell them and fix them," he replied.

"You're on," said Annie. Somehow beyond her comprehension, a social situation was developing.

"She insisted on coming to see if he had found his real owner. Three Teddies?" he said to his little girl.

It seemed to be concentrated around the Teddy Bears but it was obvious that the children's interest in each other and their toys was also extended to their parents.

"How about a Teddy Bears' picnic?" Rose suggested. "We could go to your cottage at the 'Manor', Dudley could join us."

"I live at The Lilacs now, had you forgotten. I am not allowed at the cottage."

"Was it you who beat up an evil gangster?" said the young woman with admiration.

"How brave," said the young man.

"We'll go to Alf's. John Watson looks after old Alf." All this went over the heads of the young people. They delightedly agreed to go to Alf's for a picnic.

"We'll help them along," said Annie to Rose later. "Life isn't all Teddy Bears."

No-one suspected Alf's hidden talent. He did conjuring tricks. Some didn't work out but it didn't matter as no-one knew what was supposed to happen anyway and Victoria Grace only saw a very funny man who tried to make her disappear and only produced a Teddy Bear!.

The young man (the waste of space) was called Eric and sold bells. He seemed to be full of sympathy for the widow called Violet and they agreed never to go to a country with Malaria and to meet again to discuss it.

"So much for Teddy Bears," said Annie when the party had broken up. "You just never know!" She nodded to their newly acquired mascot, she was certain he winked back!

What exactly is escorting?" Rose asked, "We seem to be asked to do a lot of it, it's quite profitable?"

"I think," answered Annie, "that it's mainly taking and fetching children from boarding school. Sometimes it would be a one-parent family or both parents abroad and dates don't fit. There must be quite a lot of it. "Yes," she added, "we could certainly take that on."

Rose consulted her lists. "This one sounds very good. My goodness this would pay the rent for months. It's taking a very ill old lady to Switzerland to visit some friends. It's only one way too. Come back when you like!"

Annie thought for some time. At last she spoke, "I wouldn't touch it with a bargepole," she said firmly. Could Rose be quite so innocent?

Rose's next remark convinced Annie that she was aware of the circumstances. "You wouldn't let your favourite pet suffer," she said. "It's only kindness."

Annie let it pass merely pointing out that they could not afford to be involved in illegality. "We have to keep our noses clean," she told Rose.

It was Friday and Annie was going to spend the weekend with the Hursts. Rose was still bent over the computer.

"Shall you be long?" asked Annie.

"About half an hour."

"Keys in the usual place then, and I might be a bit late on Monday."

"Have a good weekend."

"And you!"

Annie's weekend with the Hursts was at the Manor as Herr Gebhart was still in residence, he felt that he had had enough of England and had been offered a better position back home and he decided that they all spoke the language well enough.

Annie took Linda with her to the Manor. It was fairly chaotic there. Clare and John were wandering along with several architect friends all making different suggestions, the Hurst children had invited various friends, domestic arrangements had been taken over by a firm called 'Wedoit4u'. It all flowed over Annie's head for she had a niggling feeling that told her not to trust Rose on this occasion. But it was the weekend and she and I can talk about it next Monday.

On Monday there was a long list of possible clients, there was also a last-minute attached note which said, "Gone to Switzerland for short holiday—I have Victoria Grace". It seemed so unlikely, whatever had come over sensible Rose, certainly not a sudden need of a holiday. Annie had made her views clear and had pointed out that there was a difference between treatment of people and suffering pets when Rose had said 'you wouldn't let your favourite pet suffer'".

Dudley came in as she hovered over the phone. Annie told him her worries.

"She's gone alone Dud?"

"No, she's taken Vicky," he was laughing.

"What's so funny?" asked Annie.

"She went on the train, couldn't take the babe any other way and what she doesn't know is that Neil and I have booked flights and will be meeting her at the Swiss border," Dudley replied.

Annie joined in the laughter. Whatever Rose was up to it would soon be abandoned or denied, especially after a couple of nights in a good hotel. Annie breathed again. She looked at the list of clients and their troubles, it looked harmless enough so she, too, would have a day or two off and go shopping.

CHAPTER 4

"DOES IT MATTER WHAT I WEAR for the funeral?" Annie had asked Rose. "I've spent enough."

"Money no object and of course it matters," answered Rose who was folding up an important looking document. "The reward has come through, we've no financial worries now."

"Reward, for what?"

"For finding Miranda of course. Someone had even offered to double it. Everyone will want to talk to you or even just look."

"That was nothing, it was just chance."

Rose was indignant, "Just chance, chance! What are you talking about, chance? This is a brilliant detective agency or investigation bureau, no case is too small. This time you'd heard a rumour and naturally went to investigate. You used your intuitive and quickness of mind and decided to act. Luckily your young trainee was with you and yes, you have helped to break up a formidable international gang. Put simply—you used your Gump!"

Annie could hardly stop laughing, "It's not quite ME is it? But I'll not worry about what to wear, I've plenty of dark clothes and no-one will notice me."

"You're wrong there, everyone is longing to meet you. Your exploit with the 'Toy Boy' has grown enormously not to mention this child. What a wonderful advertising and publicity opportunity."

Annie went on laughing but one look at her wardrobe convinced her that perhaps Rose was right and a new outfit would not come amiss. But not black—certainly not black. She surprised herself therefore, when looking at and trying on various garments. One expensive black suit fitted and yes, she agreed with the assistant that "she couldn't go wrong" and after all it was for a funeral (or five). She allowed herself a more colourful and equally expensive scarf and came away from the store in a satisfied way.

She knew that there would be a necessary 'hunt' with Rose for the 'Mother of the Bride' (but not pink please Rose) and the mature look (purple perhaps) but this sophisticated suit she had done on her own!

Her new friend Janet, the vicar, had been to see her when she was still in hospital and had relieved her of her horror of five funerals.

"Leave it all to me," she had said and Annie as well as the victims' relatives and friends had been only too glad to do so.

Janet had promised to find a Methodist Minister she knew as Gordon Barnes was an active Methodist and he spoke well as Janet did. The authorities had released the bodies for burial and the victims' relatives and friends were thankful that the problems they had anticipated had been taken off their hands.

The funeral(s) went off well and Annie was quietly surrounded by protecting friends. "The Agency is not open yet," she told everybody, "but I am still working on a theory." She referred of course to the murder of the five. "I'm not sure yet," she added.

She liked the service. Janet spoke well and Annie was very impressed with Mr Anderson, the Methodist, he was sincere and whilst listening to his gentle tones her theory as to the 'why' started to form.

The village turned out in force, especially when it was known that the Wake was to be held at the Manor with no expense spared. John Watson provided this and all were grateful. Lance and the organist played a solemn duet on the grand piano, there was much applause.

Sam, viewing the food, said it was the best 'party' he'd been to but was hushed up by his siblings.

A rumour that the Manor was going to be an Old Peoples' Home got around and a number of people put their names down for when it was a going concern.

Annie was thanked for everything, even though she felt she had done nothing. Some spoke of various reunions but Annie thought these unlikely. When these relatives and friends arrived home they would try to forget the whole unhappy episode in which they felt they should never have been involved.

But Annie was still involved and was determined to find the 'key' to the mystery. A door had half opened when Mr Anderson was talking. Was it possible that honesty had killed them? Had Gordon Barnes tried to talk truth and goodness into evil he didn't understand. She would talk it over with Neil which would help to clear her mind. She would now write up the case as—now which was it? She already had the case of the lost Teddy Bear—which was number? (Oh! dear) That came after the case of the missing (or found) girl not to mention the abandoned escort.

No doubt about it, the Detective Agency was well open!

CHAPTER 5

The Case of the School Equipment

ROSE HEARD TWO SCHOOLGIRLS TALKING. The occasion was a music festival for schools. The George Pound was well represented and a local semi-boarding school called 'The Ashborne School for Girls' also had a very poor choir taking part. Rose thought that the two she heard came from this school.

"She looks a bit too posh for us." Annie was wearing her black outfit but 'posh' no thought Rose. They are the ones from the paying school.

"We can try her," the other one answered.

Rose watched as the two girls wandered over to Annie and accidentally knocked into her. Rose didn't think much of their tactics, she was also faintly suspicious of their methods. She decided to join the now socializing group.

"Introduce me to your friends," she said to Annie. They introduced themselves.

"I'm Caroline Blake and this is Iris Field. We've some bad trouble at school, my father doesn't like the publicity. He said he'd pay a private detective to sort it all out. Someone said you were one."

"A big handsome boy," said Iris Field.

'Probably Kevin,' Annie thought, she knew he was there.

"So, what's this trouble?" asked Annie.

"Someone, outside school of course, broke into the pavilion and broke up all the tennis rackets, hockey sticks and things. It must have been a burglar or a tramp or something."

"Yes," said Annie, "someone like that of course."

"Someone outside school talked and it got into the papers. The Head was furious," said Iris. "And so was Dad. He said he didn't send me to an expensive private school for its misdeeds to be shouted from the rooftops. He said he'd send me to the ghastly local school, it's called the 'George Pound', but first he'd pay for a private detective to find the culprit. Someone said you were one."

Annie swallowed hard for several reasons.

Iris said, "It was a big handsome boy said so," she told Annie. "They have chips for school dinner."

Annie swallowed again. Whatever were they up to? Later when she was telling her friend Maggie she merely answered, "I always envied them their grounds and the pavilion is almost as big as a classroom. I know Mrs Field who works in the chemist—a nice woman. So what?"

Annie answered, "Oh! They did it themselves—no doubt about that. I'll go to the school and find out why?"

"And why Father is infuriated," she added.

Annie went to the school where talks with girls and staff only confirmed her suspicions. Her final verdict was that it was plain stupidity and vindictiveness. Iris Field did what she was told by Caroline, maybe Iris would like to be somewhere else, why send her there and work in a shop? Annie thought it was all rather boring and not her sort of case at all.

One thing was obvious, all was not well in the Blake household but what was she supposed to be investigating?

The Head Mistress (this word was wrong for a start) was only interested in the reputation of the school. Annie's suggestion that she went on a long cruise was not well received. She looked hard at Annie as she said, "I shall have to expel them."

Annie felt that she would be included. It was on the tip of her tongue to say how lucky they were as they could now go to the 'George Pound'.

The Head explained as to one of poor intellect that the advantage of 'Ashborne' was their boarding facilities. For parents working abroad it was essential to have the children happy and safe.

'Maggie will soon sort these two out,' thought Annie.

The staff had told Annie that Caroline was the ringleader, it was with surprise therefore when she learned that Caroline had remained at 'Ashborne' and only Iris had left.

"I've separated them and that is enough," said the Head.

"Oh Yes," said Inspector David when Annie was telling him of this particular 'case'. "This man tried to bribe the police, I wonder what he offered the Head Mistress. And as to her—she's running around with Bassington-Crockett. Do you know him? A finger in every pie, and most of them shady!"

Annie said to Rose, "We'll reorganize our premises with you at the front entrance. I'll be the one in the back interview room. No more schoolgirls with doubtful parents thank you very much.

"OK," said Rose, "and I have the Teddy Bear?"

CHAPTER 6

⚕

THERE HAD BEEN NO DISSENTING voices when the cases of the change of use of the building had been discussed. The Old Manor, with money spent on it and there appeared to be plenty of it, would make an excellent Old Peoples' Home. There were even some discreet mutterings among the committee members suggesting that the Chairman would be needing such an establishment before very long and was therefore giving the matter preferential treatment. The hospital was also given priority for it had long since met the requirements of a health authority and the death of patients, possibly due to an outbreak of some unpleasant virus, brought the new plans to be in operation earlier than had been expected.

Annie and Rose decided that the time had come to reorganize and redecorate their premises. The place was a hive of activity. They had decided to swap offices and Kevin, who had joined them, was painting these. Bert, his father, was in what had been a small bathroom (Rose called it a wash-house!) which needed a complete update. Dudley had knocked down a wall in order to make what Rose now insisted was 'en-suite'. Rose was now going to occupy the entrance office in order to do some 'weeding' or selection of clients. An unnecessary passage would now be this 'en-suite' attachment. The bigger, lighter and altogether superior office was where the interviews would be held. Some records (Annie's old-fashioned sort) would be here for Rose's office was a technical delight (to Rose) who was muttering, "We ought to have a kitchen."

"No way," said Annie.

Annie had made her wishes well known. "We shall NOT be cooking here and smelling of chips or curry. We shall go out to lunch, when this old place is completed." She was referring to the old hospital now being transformed into a small town with shops and an arcade below and offices above.

A small sports car drew up. An attractive young lady stepped out of it and came in determinedly.

"Hello," she said to Kevin, "It's just where you said it was."

Is Kevin a dark horse? Is this his new girlfriend?

Bert said, "Nice car."

"Daddy gave it to me for my birthday, do you like it?" she asked him.

No-one stopped working so she looked around for a paintbrush, found one and joined Kevin.

"Are you a client?" Rose asked her.

"I hope so. Do you do escorting?"

"Certainly," said Annie. "Who wants to know?"

"I'm sorry, how very rude of me. I'm Beryl. Are you Mrs. Butcher?"

Annie admitted it, "Escorting, who and where?"

She added, "Although there's to be no cooking, I've nothing against a kettle. Anyone for tea now being served in the interview office?"

"The young man," she nodded towards Kevin, "recommended you. I want to work for Daddy and he is fussing so."

"In what way? Parents worry you know."

"I must have languages so he has fixed up families to stay with and colleges to attend in France, Italy, Spain and Germany, but I have to have an escort. He thought I'd refuse you see," she finished with a sigh.

"Where in France, Italy, Spain and Germany? It could be interesting."

"Oh, Paris, Rome, Madrid, Berlin . . ."

"You may not always have the same escort, we take these trips in turn," Annie said hastily before Rose bagged the lot.

"That is good of you," said Beryl, "I'll tell him, and he said he also wanted Swahili and Japanese but we'd do the European languages first.

"No trouble there," said Annie. "I speak Swahili, I was born in Kenya, and Mrs Russell's Japanese is improving daily."

Rose was about to protest but caught Annie's eye which said 'Or else! And find Japanese for Beginners on the net.' She cheered up when she remembered that Dud had mentioned what an interesting place it was and he wouldn't mind a visit there. Japan, here I come!

Dudley, unaware of this treat in store for him, kept on at his wall.

Beryl seemed greatly impressed but reluctant to go. "Do you do other things?" she asked Annie.

Annie didn't like to say 'Everything' so she replied, "Try us," then seeing Beryl's worried look, asked, "Are you in trouble?"

"Trouble! Me? Oh no, but I think Daddy is having a bit. He wouldn't do wrong of course, but he might need help. He's sort of friendly with a Police Superintendent, so I know he'd be straight."

"Yes, I'm sure too," Which Superintendent she wondered.

"What about Mummy?" Rose wanted to know.

"Mummy died last year," Beryl explained.

Annie and Rose made the necessary noises but both were touched and sorry for this solitary young person.

"Who is Daddy?" Annie asked Beryl,

Beryl stared at her. "I didn't say did I? He's Carstairs & Carstairs Exporters and Importers. He wouldn't do anything which wasn't legal or straight."

"Are we to understand that you want to be Carstairs, Carstairs & Carstairs?" suggested Annie.

"It sounds great doesn't it?" agreed Beryl.

Daddy, or Paul Carstairs, was not the tyrannical severe and unyielding Father that Beryl, unwillingly perhaps, had drawn for Annie and Rose. A widower, he had been left with a teenage much loved daughter and was trying his best to be all things for her. His father had founded the firm and he did not think it suitable for his enthusiastic young daughter to be part of it.

He was talking now to his lifelong friend Superintendent LaCoste for, yes, his police friend was Neil. He had told Neil of his schemes for keeping her occupied for a year or two. He then turned to his own troubles.

"There's evil somewhere, I know it and feel it, a mixture of bribery and keeping your mouth shut, whatever it is, its corrupt. It's all so innocent and presented to me as normal. I thought I might try that ABC place for a subtle investigation in an unsuspicious manner. What do you think? Could it be done quietly?"

"Certainly not," said Neil fiercely. "She's probably already mixed up in it whatever it is." His voice was angry and bitter.

"Really?" said Paul, "I'd only heard good of her." He looked curiously at his friend, "I've never heard you like this, what's wrong there then?"

"She'll get herself murdered one of these days. She's a widow, faithful to his memory."

"Whatever is that to do with it?" Paul was totally confused.

"Good God," he said at last, "you're in love," he laughed in delight. "At last," he added, "Tell me more."

"She refused me again last week, but I'll wear her down in the end."

Paul went on laughing, thinking, 'I'll go there this afternoon."

Beryl had left well satisfied, all was peace inside the Agency. Rose dropped what seemed to Annie to be a bombshell.

"There's a part-time temporary job going at 'Toogood & Tathem'. I thought I'd apply for it."

"Rose, Rose, my dear, aren't you happy here? Whatever should I do without you."

"Of course I'm happy, it's not that, I thought what a good place it would be to pick up tips about legal matters, save us a lot of trouble if I can get at their books and papers and things."

"It sounds positively dishonest to me and we can get anything we need. You're bound to get the job, but I'll play along if I have to. I did hear that they were involved in that case of the missing millionaire," said Annie thoughtfully

"That's what put me onto the idea, it sounded so profitable at a good interest rate."

"We'll take on anything, high interest rate or not. One thing I must stress and that is the client that does not tell the truth. We must have the facts, the true facts."

It was at this point that a woman entered and Annie came into Neil's case by another door.

'Entered' was the wrong word for this woman's dramatic and noisy shattering of their peace. She was bloody and bruised, her hair was matted with blood, and she was still in her night-wear partly covered by a torn dressing gown.

"I walked into a door," she sobbed.

"Some door," said Rose. "Don't worry Annie, Inspector David will be right over."

Annie told the woman, "We do not help people who lie to us, we know every story, this was no door!"

"He didn't do it," cried the woman.

"We've got a HE," said Annie, "it's not so static as a door."

"Ah, here he is," said Annie thankfully.

"This HE was Inspector David, he was followed by a large grinning man, "What's she done to herself this time?" he said with an extra smile for a 'good girl'.

Her dressing gown fell open and the full horror of his work was revealed.

She spoke at last, "Yes he did it, he did it," she was hysterical with her cries, "he always does it." She dropped the gown to show her savaged back.

"You bitch, you crawling, slobbering, lying slut," he went towards her but a young policeman laid a hand on the man's arm. He was fresh from defense classes. Anyone having aroused this wife-beater was doomed, he turned and struck the policeman full in the face. His nose bled, there was blood everywhere.

"Remove him, charge him—assaulting a policeman," said Inspector David, this was his very own case.

To Annie he said, "My wife is on her way, she took up helping battered women when the job at the old hospital finished."

Soon Eileen David arrived with the very large 'touch-me-if-you-dare' organizer of the home where she now worked.

The nose-blooded policeman was followed by more, enough to defend their colleague and remove the now cuffed offender.

Later Rose said, "I see what you mean, I'll be more careful in future."

"If we have a future?" said Annie. "What do I call this one, 'the non-case of the Battered Woman'. Let's get back to escorting."

"This isn't escorting," said a stranger entering at that moment, "but I believe my daughter asked if you would act for us. Would you be able to do that?" He gave Annie a very thorough searching look.

"Carstairs," he introduced himself, "Paul Carstairs."

Annie said, "of Carstairs, Carstairs & Carstairs?"

"The very one, number two in fact."

"Not escorting? Don't we get the job?" Annie asked.

"My friend, Neil LaCoste, says I'm not to ask, he also added that you were half into the case anyway. I'm very sorry but this is a curiosity visit and we can't just go on feelings and suspicions." He told of these and asked if it were possible to find out more.

Neil was right, she had somehow infiltrated his investigations.

"If you can call it that?" Neil said, entering the room

"How do you do it," he asked, "sitting here quietly in the most stunning outfit I've ever seen and solving a world wide mystery and putting an end to a word-wide circle of evil."

She answered about the outfit, she stood up and said, "I'm glad you like it." She sat down and asked, "What are you talking about? This is for Sally's wedding."

Fortunately Rose entered with coffee and was able to hear his explanation.

"That man, the one who caused the nose bleeding, we had him for police assault," he paused and took a deep breath. "He tried to bribe his way out with information, he gave it anyway. He told the story of the five murders, he'd once been a pilot, that was his place in the organization and he flew the helicopter that dropped the bodies. Poor young chap from the supermarket tried to reform them and all his housemates had to go too. We've got the lot . . ." He sat and took a coffee. He could no longer speak. At last he said, "You—yes—YOU. Please stick to Teddy Bears."

They all three looked at their mascot—a very fetching Teddy Bear.

Neil continued, "It was a huge organization, we've got the lot all right, it will be an enormous scandal, touching on some political figures and futures."

"I like the outfit!" said Rose to Annie.

Neil gave up. "I hear you had a bit of a 'do' here," he said.

"That's so," said Rose, "lots of blood."

"There's nothing we can't handle," said Annie Butcher, nodding to Teddy.

⊰⊱